AF579416

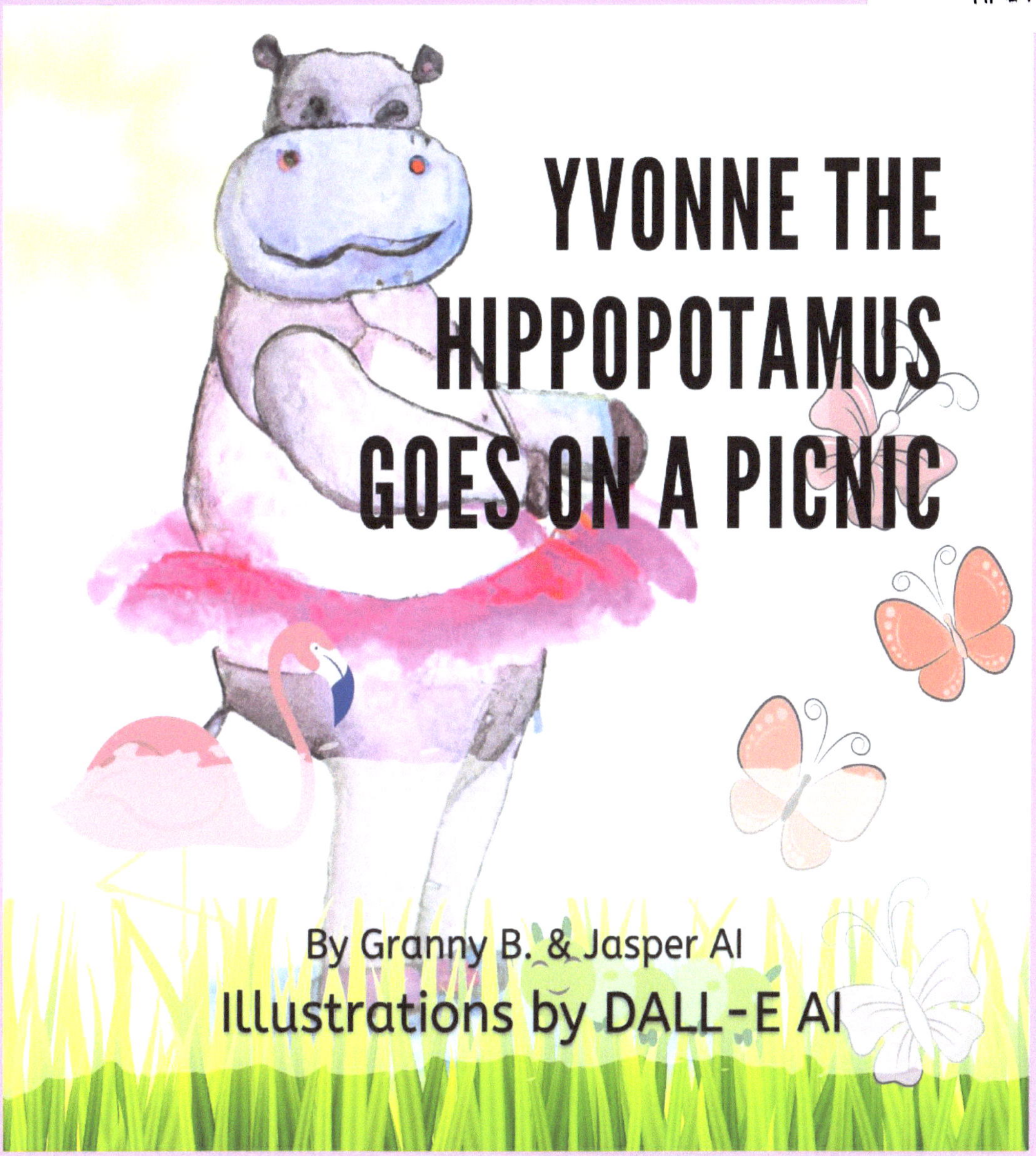

YVONNE THE HIPPOPOTAMUS GOES ON A PICNIC

By Granny B. & Jasper AI
Illustrations by DALL-E AI

YVONNE THE HIPPOPOTAMUS GOES ON A PICNIC

By Granny B. & Jasper AI
Illustrations by DALL-E AI

Copyright 2022 Granny B &
Content Creators' Group

THIS BOOK IS PARTIALLY WRITTEN WITH THE HELP OF AI.

Human & AI Creating Magic Together

To learn more about AI and how it can help humans get more done visit Grannybbooks.com

Dedicated to my Grandsons

You are the world to me.

GRANNY B.

YVONNE THE HIPPOPOTAMUS ENJOYS A DAY AT THE PARK HAVING A PICNIC WITH HER FRIENDS

Suitable for All Ages

Today's The Day!
Yvonne the Hippo wakes up
with a stretch on this
exciting sunny day!

Yvonne eats her breakfast quickly happily planning her day at the park.

Yvonne runs to her bedroom to clean it up and get packed for the fun day ahead!

Blocks go in the block box.

Yvonne puts her train set away after taking a play break.

Yvonne pins her art to the cork board, so it looks neat.

Everything is in its place! Now let's get ready for a picnic!

Yvonne packs a picnic basket.

Yvonne slathers on sunscreen to protect her skin for a long fun day at the park.

Weeeeeeeeee!!!

This is the perfect spot!

Yay! Time to eat!

Yvonne eats
watermelon.

Yvonne eats a fish
sandwich.

Let's play!

Yvonne flies a kite!

Yvonne kicks a ball!

Yvonne eats an ice
cream cone!

"Bye, I had a good time!"
Yvonne goes home.

Yvonne walks home after a fun picnic.

"What a fun day!" "I can't wait until tomorrow!" Yvonne says quietly as she falls into a deep sleep.

Good Night! The End.

THE END

Have a nice day!

www.ingramcontent.com/pod-product-compliance
Lightning Source LLC
LaVergne TN
LVHW071130160826
845679LV00005B/1239

* 9 7 9 8 8 4 5 8 4 7 3 4 8 *